THE UNMAPPED

LIVIA XIA WANG

Made with ❤ on the Notion Press Platform
www.notionpress.com

To those who seek the truth buried in shadows and time,
To the dreamers who dare to uncover the hidden stories
of our past,
And to the lovers whose timeless bond transcends all
boundaries.

May this story of love, sacrifice, and eternal connection
inspire you to find the echoes of your own heart within its
pages.

With deepest gratitude and affection,

Livia Xia Wang.

Contents

Preface

Welcome to the world of The Unmapped, a journey that spans across time, emotion, and the profound connections that bind us. This book is a labor of love, crafted with the hope of touching your heart and igniting your imagination. As you turn these pages, you will uncover a narrative that intertwines history with personal discovery, revealing truths that transcend the boundaries of time.

Published by Notion Press, this work reflects the dedication and passion that went into every word, every story, and every revelation. My goal with this book was to bring forth a tale that not only entertains but also resonates deeply with each reader, offering a glimpse into the intricate dance of fate and love.

I am immensely grateful to Notion Press for their support and belief in this project, and to you, the reader, for embarking on this journey with me. Your engagement with this story is the greatest reward and a testament to the power of storytelling.

May you find within these pages a connection to something greater, a reflection of your own experiences, and perhaps even a new perspective on the tapestry of life.

Thank you for joining me on this adventure.

With heartfelt appreciation,

Livia Xia Wang.

Acknowledgements

I would like to extend my deepest gratitude to everyone who has supported me throughout the journey of bringing this book to life. To my family and friends, your unwavering encouragement and understanding have been my greatest strength.

A special thanks to Notion Press for their exceptional support and professionalism in publishing this work. Your belief in my story has been invaluable.

To my readers, your enthusiasm and engagement are the heart of this endeavor. I am deeply appreciative of your support and hope that this book resonates with you as much as it has with me.

Thank you all for being a part of this journey.
With sincere thanks,
Livia Xia Wang.

CHAPTER I

Echoes of the Past

Sam Emmanuel Johnson had always been different. From a young age, he experienced strange phenomena that set him apart from everyone else. As he traveled, he would occasionally slip into moments from the past. These brief glimpses into history happened in a fraction of a second, unnoticed by those around him. Sam never spoke of these experiences, keeping them a secret even from his family. In his sleep, he continued to experience these "time slips," but he always knew that these events were from the past and that there was no need to worry.

He tried to capture what he saw in a diary, but his poor drawing skills made his sketches indecipherable to anyone else. His family often teased him about his strange drawings, except for his mother, who saw something special in him. Seeing him disheartened by the teasing, she enrolled him in a drawing class, where he learned to express his visions more clearly.

Sam Emmanuel Johnson was a tall, strikingly handsome young man with features. His demeanor was introverted, creating an air of mystery around him. He lived in a world of his own, where his only companions were his drawing books and a palette of colors. While others found joy in social interactions, Sam found solace in his art, channeling his thoughts and emotions into each stroke of the brush.

His classmates often viewed him as strange, a loner who kept to himself and never engaged in the typical banter of youth. Even when approached with questions, Sam remained distant, offering no answers, leaving others puzzled by his silence. Yet, despite his aloofness, there was no denying his intelligence. Sam excelled in his studies, demonstrating a sharp mind, keen discipline, and a brave, determined spirit that set him apart from everyone else. His courage wasn't the loud, obvious kind, but rather a quiet resolve that guided him through life's challenges.

Though his peers may have seen him as an enigma, his teachers recognized a quiet brilliance in Sam. He was obedient, respectful, and dedicated to his work, qualities that set him apart in the classroom. To them, Sam was not just a student, but a gifted individual with a unique perspective on the world—one that he expressed through his art, rather than words.

In a world where he was often misunderstood, Sam's artistic talents, academic prowess, and unwavering determination became his sanctuary, allowing him to navigate life on his own terms, even if it meant walking a path less traveled.

As Sam honed his artistic skills, his fascination with the past grew. He pursued a career in archaeology, hoping to uncover the mysteries that had always seemed to call out to him. While working in the archaeological department, he dedicated himself to studying ancient civilizations and their hidden secrets.

One day, while on vacation, Sam decided to visit a remote village nestled halfway up a mountain—a place that had often appeared in his time slips. The village, with its picturesque scenery and ancient history, felt like a familiar yet unexplored chapter in his life, one that seemed to stretch back centuries. As he neared his destination, Sam felt a strange sense of purpose, as if he was meant to be there.

Upon arriving, he experienced a vision more vivid than any before. He witnessed a brutal murder, the victim's clothes indicating a time over six hundred years ago. Startled, he quickly sketched what he had seen, noting every detail. When he reached his cottage, Sam questioned the staff about the history of the place, asking if anyone had ever felt negative energies. The room boy assured him that the village had been peaceful for over a century.

Determined to find answers, Sam wandered through the village, seeking anyone who could provide clues about his vision. He encountered an old man selling mangoes by the roadside and inquired about any strange occurrences in the village's history. The old man had no knowledge of such events.

As Sam walked back to his resort, he stumbled upon a spot that felt eerily familiar. As he stepped into the area, he was suddenly transported back in time. He witnessed the continuation of the brutal scene he had seen earlier. The victim, whom everyone thought was dead, had been buried alive beneath the ground where Sam now stood. In that moment, Sam felt a suffocating sensation, as if all his energy was being drained away. He struggled to breathe and felt utterly paralyzed, but he managed to regain control and return to the present.

As he returned to the present, a lingering coldness clung to his skin, as if the past had left its mark not only on his mind but on his very soul. Shaken, Sam questioned the villagers again, but no one knew of any mystical occurrences in the village's past.

It became clear to him that these visions were not random; they were connected to him in some profound way. As he stood on the threshold of the unknown, Sam realized that the past was not just a distant memory—it was a part of him, calling him to uncover the truth hidden beneath the surface. And so, with a mix of dread and determination, he prepared to delve deeper into the mysteries of time, knowing that his journey had only just begun.

CHAPTER II

The Unearthed Secrets

Back in his cottage, Sam couldn't shake the feeling that the village held more secrets than its picturesque appearance suggested. Determined to uncover the truth, he decided to dig deeper—both figuratively and literally. He visited the local archives and museums, seeking any record of unexplained phenomena or significant historical events. However, his inquiries were met with polite but unhelpful responses, as the village's history seemed uneventful on the surface.

Unfazed, Sam decided to investigate the location from his vision—the site where the man had been buried alive. Armed with his archaeological tools, he returned to the spot under the cover of darkness, his heart pounding with anticipation. As he dug carefully, he soon unearthed an ornately carved box, locked and well-preserved. Sam felt a thrill of discovery rather than fear; this box could hold the key to understanding his visions.

Returning to his cottage, he examined the box. The carvings were intricate, depicting scenes of daily life from an ancient era and symbols that hinted at a culture rich in tradition. Curious, Sam contacted his colleague, Professor Eliza Hayes, an expert in ancient artifacts. With her extensive experience and profound knowledge, Eliza was someone Sam relied on deeply. Her calm demeanor had a way of easing his often-introverted nature, and they shared a strong intellectual bond. Sam saw her as a big sister, and her cool-minded behavior had significantly influenced him, making their collaboration both effective andharmonious.

Eliza arrived in the village the next day.

Together, they studied the box. Sam enquired while opening the box and revealing the carvings, "Eliza, take a look at this. The carvings are so detailed—like a snapshot of life from a different era. What do you make of them?"

Eliza examined the carvings closely and responded, "These symbols resemble those found in cultures known for elaborate burial rites. This box could have been used to carry significant items meant to accompany someone into the afterlife."

"I had a feeling this was more than just an ordinary artifact. There's something almost... familiar about it." Sam remarked with curiosity. His face is a mix of curiosity and contemplation. His brow furrows slightly, and his eyes narrow as if he's trying to piece together a puzzle in his mind. There's a hint of a smile, almost as if he's on the brink of a significant realization but can't quite grasp it.

Eliza listens intently, her face showing a keen interest. Her eyes are wide, and there's a soft smile on her lips as she notes, "That's not surprising. Many archaeologists and historians find personal connections to their discoveries." She's slightly nodding, her expression one of understanding and insight. As she asks about the excavation, there's a slight lift in her eyebrows, reflecting her genuine curiosity.

"No, actually." Sam revealed, his expression shifts to one of mild disappointment. His eyes momentarily drop as if searching for answers. His lips press together in a thin line, showing that he wishes there was more to uncover, but he's resigned to the fact that there wasn't.

Their research led them to revisit the excavation site. This time, they carefully expanded their dig, revealing a stone-lined burial chamber. Inside, they found a beautifully crafted coffin, untouched by time. As they opened it, they were astonished to see a remarkably well-preserved body, as if the person had been embalmed with an advanced technique that had prevented decomposition.

The body, dressed in rich garments, appeared to belong to someone of high status. Alongside it, they found various personal belongings: jewelry, a small dagger, and a collection of scrolls. These artifacts suggested the deceased was a person of importance, possibly a leader or a revered figure in their society.

"That's a profound observation. The artifacts we find can often evoke deep emotions. The jewelry and dagger suggest this person held a significant role. We should document everything meticulously." Eliza observed, her face shows deep thoughtfulness. Her eyes are focused, and her lips are slightly pursed as she contemplates the significance of what they've found. There's a seriousness in her expression, emphasizing the importance of their work. As she mentions documenting everything, her brows lift slightly, indicating her dedication and attention to detail.

"Absolutely. I want to understand more about who they were. This is more than just a historical find—it's a part of the story I've been glimpsing in my time slips." Sam agreed, his expression is one of determination and intrigue. His eyes have a spark of excitement mixed with a hint of nostalgia as he connects the artifacts to his experiences. His mouth forms a small, firm smile, reflecting his resolve to uncover more.

"It's fascinating how your experiences seem to align with our discoveries. The connection between your visions and these artifacts might reveal deeper insights into their culture." Eliza noted, her expression was one of curiosity and encouragement. Her eyes widen slightly, and there's a gentle smile, showing her genuine interest in Sam's unique connection to the artifacts. Her head tilts slightly as she speaks, indicating her deep engagement in the conversation.

"I think so too. Each detail we uncover feels like a piece of a larger puzzle. It's as if these artifacts are telling a story that I've only begun to understand." Sam responded, his face reflected a mixture of awe and introspection. His eyes narrow as if he's trying to piece together a complex puzzle. There's a slight furrow in his brow, and his lips part slightly as if he's on the verge of a significant realization. His expression conveys both wonder and a sense of urgency.

"And the fact that the body and belongings are so well-preserved might offer us clues about their burial practices and societal values. We need to be thorough in our analysis." Eliza added, her expression was serious and focused. Her eyes narrow as she emphasized the importance of their work. Her lips pressed into a thin line, and there's a slight nod, reflecting her commitment to approaching the discovery with the respect and care it deserved.

"Definitely. I'm eager to see how this find connects with the history I've been exploring. It's not just about unearthing artifacts but uncovering a personal link to the past." Sam concurred, his expression was one of deep resolve. His eyes were intense, reflecting his desire to understand the deeper connection between the artifacts and his own experiences. His jaw was set, and there's a slight, determined smile, showing that he's fully committed to this journey of discovery.

"Indeed. This discovery is shaping up to be not just a significant archaeological find but also a meaningful connection to your past experiences. Let's proceed with care and respect for this remarkable piece of history." Eliza agreed, her expression softened slightly, showing a deep reverence for the history they were uncovering. Her eyes reflected a sense of awe, and her lips curved into a small, respectful smile. There's a sense of shared understanding between her and Sam, underscored by a mutual respect for the past they were uncovering.

As Sam and Eliza documented their findings, they felt a deep sense of connection to the past. There were no signs of curses or malevolent forces, just the serene and respectful preservation of a life once lived.

Word of their discovery spread quickly through the village. The locals, initially wary, became intrigued and proud of their newly uncovered heritage. The village head, who had initially been concerned about the disturbance, now saw the potential for this discovery to bring positive attention and historical significance to the village.

Sam and Eliza carefully cataloged the items and arranged for the proper authorities to assist in preserving and studying the site. As they continued their work, Sam felt a sense of closure. The visions that had haunted him were not curses or warnings but a call to uncover and honor the past.

Through this journey, Sam realized that his experiences were a gift, guiding him to rediscover a forgotten piece of history. The preserved body and the artifacts told a story of a once-thriving community, rich in culture and tradition. It was a legacy that deserved to be remembered and respected.

As the excavation came to a close, Sam felt a peaceful resolution. He had fulfilled a mysterious and long-forgotten duty, bringing to light the life and times of an ancient individual. This experience deepened his appreciation for history and the mysteries of the past, leaving him eager for future explorations and discoveries.

CHAPTER III

The Silent Histories

With the discovery of the burial chamber, Sam and Eliza found themselves at the center of growing interest from both the academic community and the local villagers. The unearthed artifacts and the well-preserved body had sparked a flurry of excitement and curiosity. The media began to cover the find, and a team of experts arrived to assist in the excavation and study of the site.

As they continued their work, Sam and Eliza noticed that the items in the burial chamber hinted at a rich and complex culture. The scrolls, once carefully unrolled and preserved, revealed a series of beautifully written texts. Eliza, with her knowledge of ancient languages, began to translate them. The texts told stories of a once-thriving civilization that had valued knowledge, art, and spiritual practices. They also contained references to a wise leader who had guided the community through prosperous times.

Intrigued by these revelations, Sam and Eliza decided to delve deeper into the village's history. They consulted with local historians and elders, hoping to uncover oral traditions or folklore that might align with the newly discovered artifacts. They discovered that the village's history had been largely oral, passed down through generations. While much of it had faded over time, some stories hinted at a once-great leader who had mysteriously vanished, leaving behind a legacy that had been forgotten.

As Sam and Eliza pieced together the fragments of the past, they uncovered a fascinating theory: the leader they had found buried in the chamber might have been a central figure in the village's history, perhaps even its founder. The discovery of such a well-preserved body suggested that this person had been of immense importance, possibly revered as a spiritual or political leader.

Their investigation also led them to a series of ancient ruins located deeper in the mountains, previously thought to be insignificant. With the help of the new expert team, they explored these ruins and found evidence of a sophisticated society. The architecture, inscriptions, and artifacts suggested a community that had once flourished with advanced knowledge and cultural achievements.

As they explored the ruins, Sam began to feel an eerie sense of familiarity. He realized that some of the locations matched the places he had seen in his visions. This realization brought a mix of excitement and unease; his time slips were not just random occurrences but seemed to be guiding him toward uncovering this lost history.

The more they uncovered, the more questions arose. What had happened to this once-great civilization? Why had the leader been buried with such care, yet left forgotten? And why did Sam have these visions connecting him to this place and time?

As the team continued their excavation and study, they began to notice subtle indications of an abrupt end to the civilization. The scrolls mentioned a sudden and mysterious decline, possibly due to environmental changes or conflict. However, there was no clear explanation, leaving much of the past shrouded in mystery.

Sam and Eliza decided to document their findings meticulously, planning to publish a comprehensive study on this newly discovered civilization, a few kilometres away from the tomb, they uncovered before. They hoped to shed light on this forgotten chapter of history and perhaps inspire further research. Meanwhile, the villagers, proud of their heritage, began to embrace the findings, seeing them as a connection to a grand and noble past.

As the chapter closes, Sam reflects on his journey. His unique experiences and the visions that had led him here were beginning to make sense. He felt a deep connection to the past, not as a mere observer but as a custodian of history. The silent histories of the village were now being heard, and Sam knew that his role in uncovering them was far from over. There were still many unanswered questions and untold stories waiting to be discovered, and he was determined to continue exploring them.

CHAPTER IV

Echoes Through Time

The excavation of the burial site had become more than a professional endeavor for Sam. Each artifact he touched seemed to evoke profound emotions, stirring within him a mixture of sadness and sorrow. The once-innocuous objects—a bejeweled dagger, intricately designed jewelry, and personal trinkets—now held a weight far beyond their physical form. As he handled these items, he often found himself overcome with an unexpected wave of weeping, his emotions raw and uncontrollable.

It was as if the artifacts were not merely remnants of a lost civilization but keys to his own past. Sam began to understand that these objects were connected to him on a deeply personal level. His experiences were no longer just about uncovering history; they were about discovering a part of himself he hadn't fully understood.

One evening, as the sun dipped below the horizon, casting a warm glow over the excavation site, Sam picked up a beautifully crafted sword. The blade was intricately adorned with symbols and runes that seemed to pulse with an ancient energy. As his fingers brushed against the cold metal, a familiar sensation swept over him—a rush of disorientation followed by a deep, immersive vision.

In an instant, Sam found himself transported to a different time and place. He was no longer at the excavation site but in a vibrant, ancient landscape. The sky was painted with hues of twilight, and the air was filled with the sounds of distant, rhythmic drumming. He was in the midst of a grand, open field surrounded by towering mountains and lush greenery.

Before him stood a figure, clad in regal attire, with a face painted a striking shade of blue. The figure was holding a sword similar to the one Sam had just touched. They were engaged in a mock duel, their movements graceful and fluid. The blue-faced figure looked at Sam with a mixture of recognition and amusement.

Sam's heart raced as he realized the figure was someone he knew—an older version of himself? His alter ego, an incarnation from the past, was training or playing in a way that was strangely familiar yet surreal. The duel was not violent but rather a dance of skill and camaraderie, a demonstration of a bond forged in another era.

As they sparred, Sam felt a surge of memories flooding back—moments of joy, intense focus, and a profound sense of connection. This was a part of his past he had never lived but somehow deeply resonated with him. The blue-faced figure seemed to guide him, not just in combat but in understanding his role and purpose in this ancient world.

The vision gradually faded, and Sam found himself back at the excavation site, the sword still in his hand. His breath came in ragged gasps, and his emotions were a whirlwind of awe and confusion. He realized with pain that each time slips he experienced, were not merely glimpses into history but intimate encounters with his own past lives.

Later that evening, Sam sat down with Eliza in his cottage, still grappling with the intensity of his latest vision. He explained the details, his voice trembling slightly as he recounted the sight of the blue-faced figure.

"Eliza, it wasn't just a vision. It felt like... like I was actually there, living that moment. And the figure—he was holding the same sword. It's as if I was dueling with myself from another time," Sam confided, his eyes searching hers for some understanding.

Eliza listened intently, her usual calm demeanor providing Sam with a grounding presence. "That's remarkable, Sam. The blue-faced figure—could it be an ancient version of you? Perhaps a memory from a past life?"

Sam nodded, the thought both terrifying and exhilarating. "I think so. Everything felt so real. I recognized the surroundings, the rhythm of the drums… It's like I've been there before, but in another lifetime."

Eliza leaned back, her brow furrowed in thought. "If that's true, then these artifacts aren't just historical pieces. They're fragments of your past, keys to unlocking who you were and the role you played in that time. We need to explore this further, piece together the story."

"I've already started researching," Sam replied, his voice gaining strength. "I couldn't find any references to a blue-faced warrior in any ancient texts. We need to dig deeper."

Eliza smiled, a hint of admiration in her eyes. "I'll help you with that. We're not just unearthing history, Sam; we're uncovering your history. This could change everything we know about the connection between past lives and artifacts."

As they continued to talk, Sam felt a renewed sense of purpose. His connection with the artifacts had taken on a new dimension. They were not just relics but fragments of his own journey through time. He needed to uncover more about this past life, to understand the role he had played and how it influenced his present.

Determined to delve deeper, Sam and Eliza spent the next few weeks poring over ancient records and texts, piecing together the significance of the blue-faced figure and the role Sam had once played. The artifacts were becoming a bridge between his present and past, revealing a narrative that spanned centuries.

As Sam continued to explore these connections, he realized that his mission was evolving. It was no longer just about unearthing the history of a forgotten civilization but also about understanding and reconciling with his own place in that history. Each artifact, each vision, was guiding him toward a greater understanding of his own identity and purpose.

With renewed resolve, Sam prepared for the next steps of his journey, knowing that the answers he sought lay not only in the artifacts themselves but in the deep, emotional connections they evoked. His path was becoming clearer, and he was ready to face whatever revelations awaited him.

CHAPTER V

The Unexpected Manuscript

Determined to unravel the mysteries of his past, Sam visited the local history museum. The museum housed an extensive collection of historical texts, artifacts, and documents. Sam spent hours sifting through dusty volumes and ancient manuscripts, searching for anything that might shed light on the civilization he was uncovering.

As he was engrossed in his research, a peculiar event occurred. A book fell from one of the shelves, landing softly on the floor. It wasn't a history book but a leather-bound volume with an ornate cover, decorated with intricate patterns. The title, "Chronicles of the Lost Realm," suggested a narrative rather than a historical account.

Sam picked up the fallen book, his curiosity piqued. "Chronicles of the Lost Realm?" he mused, turning the book over in his hands. "This doesn't belong here. How did it end up falling? And why now?" The ornate cover seemed to shimmer under the dim light, as if it held secrets waiting to be unraveled. "This isn't just a book, is it?" Sam thought, feeling a strange pull toward it. "It's almost like it chose me."

His fingers traced the intricate patterns on the cover, a sense of familiarity washing over him. Settling into a quiet corner, Sam opened the book to the first page. The text was written in an elegant script, recounting tales of a once-great civilization.

The book unfolded the tale of a long-forgotten kingdom that thrived in a time when legends were born. This kingdom, nestled in fertile valleys and surrounded by majestic mountains, was a haven of peace and prosperity. Under King Karthikeya's rule, the land experienced a golden era—a time when the sun shone brighter, the rivers ran clearer, and the people lived in harmony with nature.

King Karthikeya was a ruler unlike any other. Tall and broad-shouldered, he carried the weight of his kingdom with a quiet strength that inspired loyalty. His amber eyes held the wisdom of a thousand lifetimes, and his voice, though often soft-spoken, commanded the attention of all who heard it. He was known not only for his strategic mind and prowess in battle but also for his profound sense of justice. The animals of the kingdom, too, sensed his benevolent nature, often approaching him without fear, as if recognizing a kindred spirit.

But it was his heart that truly defined him. His love for his queen, Suvarna, was legendary, a story whispered across the kingdom in tones of reverence. Queen Suvarna was the jewel of the realm, a woman of unparalleled grace and kindness. Her beauty, with dark flowing hair, luminous skin, and eyes that sparkled with inner light, was matched by a soul shaped by empathy and wisdom. She was a queen who was not just a ruler's wife but a mother to the entire kingdom. Her presence could ease the troubles of the heart, and her words were a balm to the soul.

When the news of Queen Suvarna's pregnancy spread, the entire kingdom vibrated with joy. The streets filled with celebrations, and the people offered prayers for the safe arrival of the royal heir. The kingdom had long awaited this moment, and now, with the promise of a new life, the future seemed even more golden.

The day Siddharth was born was like no other. The sky was clear, the sun shone brilliantly, and a gentle breeze carried the scent of blooming flowers. When the first cry of the newborn prince echoed through the palace, the entire kingdom exhaled a collective sigh of relief and joy. Celebrations followed, with feasts, music, and dancing in the streets.

Prince Siddharth was no ordinary child. His skin was soft and fair, his eyes a deep, soulful brown. There was an aura about him, a presence that was felt by all who came near. The black scar on his left hand, shaped like a butterfly, became a symbol of the prince's unique destiny. The people of the kingdom believed that Siddharth was destined for greatness, that he would bring about a new era of prosperity and peace.

As Siddharth grew, he confirmed the kingdom's hopes. He was not only beautiful but also intelligent and curious, with a kindness that mirrored his mother's and a strength that echoed his father's. He was the apple of everyone's eye, a beacon of hope for the future.

As Sam read about Siddharth's early life, he felt a deepening connection to the story. The details of the prince's birth and the unique scar resonated with him, revealing hidden fragments of his own forgotten past. The narrative of Siddharth mirrored the feelings and visions Sam had encountered during his time slips, deepening his intrigue.

The book also mentioned a "chosen one" who would reconnect with the past through mystical relics, uncovering hidden truths and fulfilling a great destiny. This figure was prophesied to bring balance and understanding, bridging the gap between the past and the present. The description suggested that the artifacts Sam had found were not merely historical treasures but crucial pieces in understanding his own purpose.

Realizing the significance of the book, Sam felt it guiding him toward a deeper understanding of his role and the connections between his present and past lives. He decided to take the book with him, feeling an almost magnetic bond to its contents. The museum staff had no record of the book's origin, which only heightened the mystery.

As he left the museum, Sam felt a renewed sense of purpose. The book had opened a new chapter in his quest, blending history with personal discovery. He knew that each revelation would bring him closer to understanding the full extent of his connection to the past and the destiny that awaited him.

CHAPTER VI

Bonds of Friendship

In the heart of the kingdom, the bond between Prince Siddharth and Veer Tej was a testament to the power of friendship that transcended social status and expectation. As Sam delved deeper into the book, he found himself captivated by the story of the two boys who, despite their different backgrounds, formed an unbreakable connection.

Prince Siddharth, born into royalty, was every bit the image of a future king. From a young age, his presence was commanding yet gentle. His features were a reflection of his parents' love—strong, with a soft kindness in his deep brown eyes that seemed to carry the wisdom of his lineage. His hair, dark and thick, framed a face that was both regal and approachable. Even as a child, there was an air of nobility about him, a natural grace that set him apart. But what endeared him to those around him was not just his royal demeanor; it was his warmth, his genuine care for others, and his curiosity about the world.

Veer Tej, on the other hand, was the son of the kingdom's military captain, a position of great honor and responsibility, though not one of nobility. Veer Tej was a striking boy, with a lean, athletic build that hinted at the rigorous training he would one day undergo under his father's watchful eye. His eyes were a piercing blue, sharp and alert, always flickering with a sense of mischief and curiosity. His hair, lighter than Siddharth's, often fell into his face, giving him a slightly rebellious look that matched his adventurous spirit. Veer was known for his quick wit and boundless energy, traits that sometimes got him into trouble, especially when he and Siddharth pushed the boundaries of what was allowed.

Captain Tej, Veer's father, was a man of discipline and honor, known throughout the kingdom as a formidable leader and a loyal servant of the crown. He was tall and broad-shouldered, with a stern countenance that rarely betrayed emotion. His hair, though starting to gray, was kept short and neat, and his face bore the lines of a man who had seen many battles. Captain Tej's eyes were the same piercing blue as his son's, though they often held a seriousness that reflected his position and the weight of his responsibilities. He was a man who believed in order and structure, principles he sought to instill in Veer from a young age. Despite his strictness, there was no doubt that he loved his son dearly, though his affection was often shown through firm guidance rather than gentle words.

The friendship between Siddharth and Veer Tej blossomed from the moment they met. Veer, despite his father's rigid expectations, was drawn to Siddharth's kindness and natural leadership. Siddharth, in turn, found in Veer a friend who was unafraid to challenge him, to push him beyond the confines of royal protocol. Together, they explored the vast palace grounds, turning every corner and corridor into a new adventure. Siddharth's gentle nature balanced Veer's fiery spirit, and in return, Veer brought out a sense of adventure in the prince that might have otherwise remained dormant.

Their education, which began at the age of five under the guidance of the kingdom's most esteemed scholars, was a shared journey. Siddharth and Veer tackled their lessons together, their minds as eager as their bodies were restless. Where Siddharth excelled in understanding the complexities of statecraft and diplomacy, Veer showed a natural aptitude for strategy and combat, no doubt a trait inherited from his father. But it wasn't just academic pursuits that bonded them; it was the camaraderie they shared, the way they could laugh off a difficult lesson or encourage each other when one struggled.

Veer's position as the captain's son came with its own set of challenges. Captain Tej was strict, imposing rules that sometimes felt stifling to a boy as spirited as Veer. But Siddharth had a way of easing those burdens, convincing Veer to join him in bending the rules for the sake of a little fun. Whether it was sneaking out to explore the nearby forests or devising new games to play in the palace gardens, the two boys found joy in each other's company, their laughter echoing through the halls of the palace. Veer often faced his father's stern reprimands for these adventures, but the thrill of friendship made every scolding worth it.

The bond between Siddharth and Veer did not go unnoticed. King Karthikeya and Queen Suvarna watched their son's friendship with a mixture of pride and warmth. They saw in Veer a boy who, despite his different background, was a true friend to their son—loyal, brave, and kind. The Queen, especially, admired Veer's humility and politeness, qualities that made him a welcome presence in the royal household. Even Captain Tej, though often disapproving of his son's escapades, could not deny the positive influence Siddharth had on Veer. He saw in the prince a future king who would lead with both strength and compassion, and he was grateful that his son had such a companion.

As Sam read on, he couldn't help but feel a deep connection to the story of Siddharth and Veer. Their friendship, built on trust, mutual respect, and a shared sense of adventure, resonated with him in a way that was both comforting and inspiring. He realized that the bonds of friendship were not just about shared experiences, but about the way those experiences shaped and strengthened the people involved. In Siddharth and Veer, Sam saw a reflection of the connections in his own life, and it made the story of the lost kingdom feel all the more personal and profound.

CHAPTER VII

The Warriors' Path

The sun had just begun its ascent, casting a golden hue over the sprawling training grounds of the lost kingdom. The air was thick with the scent of earth and sweat, as the rhythmic thuds of fists against wooden dummies echoed across the field. Siddharth and Veer Tej, now eighteen, stood at the center of this ancient arena, their bodies honed from years of relentless training, their minds sharp and focused.

Siddharth, with his tall, commanding presence, had grown into a figure that exuded both strength and serenity. His dark hair, now longer, was tied back, revealing a face that had matured into a mask of calm determination. His eyes, deep and thoughtful, held the wisdom of his lineage but also the fire of his youthful spirit. Every movement he made was precise, a reflection of his years spent mastering the arts of combat, yoga, and meditation.

Beside him stood Veer Tej, lean and agile, with a spark in his blue eyes that spoke of both mischief and fierce loyalty. His lighter hair, tousled from the morning's exertions, fell into his face, but he paid it no mind. Where Siddharth was composed, Veer was quick and decisive, his body coiled like a spring, ready to strike at a moment's notice. The two moved in tandem, their training having forged a bond so deep that they could anticipate each other's actions without a word.

As they paused to catch their breath, the King himself, clad in the royal blue of his station, observed from a distance, a proud smile playing on his lips. King Karthikeya had watched his son and Veer grow from boys into warriors, and the pride he felt in their accomplishments was immeasurable. These were not just his son and his son's friend; they were the future of his kingdom, a future he knew was in capable hands.

Siddharth turned to Veer, a smirk tugging at the corners of his mouth. "You're getting slow, Veer. I thought you were supposed to keep me on my toes."

Veer, panting slightly, grinned back, wiping the sweat from his brow. "I'm only going easy on you, Siddharth. Wouldn't want to bruise that royal ego of yours."

They both laughed, a sound that cut through the morning air like a song. Their banter was light, but the bond between them was unbreakable, forged in the fires of their shared experiences and relentless training.

"Do you ever wonder," Siddharth said, more serious now, "what it would be like if we weren't bound by the expectations of the court? If we were just...free?"

Veer's expression softened. "Sometimes. But then I think about what we've been given—the opportunities, the training, the chance to make a difference. And I realize that we're exactly where we're supposed to be."

Siddharth nodded, his gaze drifting toward the horizon. "You're right. But sometimes, I can't help but feel that the weight of our roles will only grow heavier. And with it, the challenges we'll face."

Veer placed a hand on Siddharth's shoulder, a gesture of reassurance. "Whatever comes our way, we'll face it together. We've been through too much to let anything—or anyone—come between us."

Their words hung in the air, a silent vow that neither had to speak aloud. They had been inseparable since childhood, their bond only growing stronger with time. But with their rise in prominence came inevitable rivalries. The sons of ministers and nobles, feeling overshadowed by the duo's prowess, had begun to sow seeds of discord, their envy threatening to disrupt the harmony that Siddharth and Veer had worked so hard to maintain.

Later that day, as they practiced their swordsmanship, one of these rivals, a tall, broad-shouldered noble named Arjun, approached them. His eyes gleamed with barely concealed resentment as he watched the two spar.

"You two think you're invincible, don't you?" Arjun's voice was sharp, his words laced with bitterness.

Veer paused, lowering his sword. "We don't think we're invincible, Arjun. We just train hard, like everyone else."

"Harder than everyone else," Siddharth added, his tone even but firm. "If that bothers you, perhaps you should focus on your own training instead of worrying about ours."

Arjun's jaw tightened, but before he could respond, Veer stepped forward, his expression challenging. "If you have something to prove, Arjun, why don't you step into the ring?"

Arjun's eyes flickered with hesitation, but his pride wouldn't let him back down. "Fine. Let's see if your training really makes you as strong as you think."

The two squared off, and for a moment, the world around them seemed to hold its breath. Siddharth watched closely, his hand instinctively resting on the hilt of his own sword, ready to intervene if things went too far.

The clash was swift and intense. Veer's speed was matched by Arjun's brute strength, but it quickly became apparent that Veer's years of disciplined training gave him the upper hand. With a final, decisive move, Veer disarmed Arjun, sending his sword clattering to the ground.

Arjun stood there, breathing heavily, his face flushed with both exertion and embarrassment. Veer, ever gracious in victory, offered a hand to his fallen opponent. "You're strong, Arjun. But strength isn't everything. Keep training, and you'll get there."

Arjun hesitated, then reluctantly took Veer's hand, allowing himself to be pulled to his feet. "You're right," he muttered, though his tone lacked the usual bravado. "I'll work harder."

As Arjun walked away, Siddharth turned to Veer, a smile tugging at his lips. "That was...unexpectedly diplomatic of you."

Veer shrugged, sheathing his sword. "We have enough enemies outside these walls. No point in making more within them."

Siddharth nodded, his respect for his friend growing even more. "You've always had a way of seeing the bigger picture, Veer. It's one of the reasons I'm glad to have you by my side."

The sun dipped lower in the sky as the day wore on, but for Siddharth and Veer, the challenges were far from over. Their bond, however, remained their greatest strength—a bond forged not just in the fires of battle, but in the understanding, trust, and respect they held for each other.

As Sam read these passages, he felt a deep resonance with the story. The dynamic between Siddharth and Veer—their unyielding friendship in the face of growing rivalries and the pressures of their roles—echoed the struggles and relationships in his own life. Each word seemed to pull him further into the world of the lost kingdom, making him feel as though he was walking the very path that Siddharth and Veer had trodden centuries before.

CHAPTER VIII

Bonds Beyond Brotherhood

The days in the kingdom were growing longer as the responsibilities of adulthood began to weigh on Siddharth and Veer Tej. The once carefree days of their youth had given way to the complexities of leadership and duty. Siddharth, now fully embracing his role as the future king, exuded a quiet authority that made him beloved by his people. Veer, on the other hand, had become a strategic genius, his mind as sharp as the sword he wielded with unmatched skill. Together, they were the embodiment of strength and unity, a living symbol of the kingdom's future.

The sun had nearly set, painting the sky in shades of deep orange and purple. Siddharth and Veer found themselves by the lake, a place they often retreated to when the pressures of their roles became too heavy. The stillness of the water mirrored the peace they felt in each other's company—a rare solace in the midst of their demanding lives.

Siddharth stared out at the water, his thoughts a tangle of duties and desires. The weight of their duties had been particularly heavy lately, and they sought solace in each other's company.

Veer glanced at Siddharth, who was lost in thought. "Sometimes, it feels like we're just pieces in a grand game, doesn't it? Moving here and there according to the whims of fate."

Siddharth sighed, his gaze fixed on the horizon. "Yes, but it's not just the game. It's the feeling that no matter what we do, we're always being watched, always being judged."

Veer tilted his head, considering Siddharth's words. "And you think that's different from what we'd face as ordinary men?"

Siddharth turned to Veer, his eyes reflecting a mix of melancholy and determination. "It's not just about the scrutiny. It's the loss of freedom—the ability to act on our own desires without considering how it will affect our roles, our people."

Veer nodded slowly, understanding the burden Siddharth felt. "You're right. Sometimes I wonder what it would be like to live a simpler life. But then I remember that we have each other, and that makes all the difference."

Siddharth's expression softened. "You make it easier, Veer. Even in the midst of all these responsibilities, your presence is a reminder that there's more to life than the weight of a crown."

Veer smiled warmly, placing a reassuring hand on Siddharth's shoulder. "And no matter what comes our way, we'll face it together. That's something no crown or title can change."

Siddharth looked at Veer with gratitude, feeling a sense of peace in their shared moment. "Yes, together. That's all I need to keep going."

They sat in silence for a moment, the air between them thick with unspoken emotions. The connection they shared had always been special, but as they had grown, so too had the depth of their bond. There was a comfort in their silence, a wordless understanding that only they shared.

Finally, Veer broke the silence, his voice soft. "Siddharth, there's something I've been meaning to say... but I've been afraid."

Siddharth's heart skipped a beat. He could feel the tension in Veer's words, the hesitation that made his voice tremble ever so slightly. "What is it?"

Veer hesitated, then took a deep breath. "We've always been more than just friends, haven't we? I mean... there's something between us, something that goes beyond just friendship."

Siddharth's chest tightened as he met Veer's gaze. There, in the depths of Veer's blue eyes, he saw the same feelings that had been swirling inside him for so long—feelings he had been too scared to acknowledge. "Yes," he whispered, his voice barely audible. "I think there has been for a long time."

Veer exhaled, a mixture of relief and fear washing over him. "I didn't want to make things complicated, but I can't ignore it anymore. I... I care about you, Siddharth. More than I should."

Siddharth reached out, his hand finding Veer's and clasping it tightly. "You don't have to apologize for how you feel, Veer. I care about you too... more than I've ever cared about anyone."

The words hung between them, a fragile truth finally laid bare. The tension that had been building for years seemed to dissipate, replaced by a quiet understanding that this was not just friendship; this was love. Pure, unspoken, and profound.

"We can't let anyone know," Siddharth said softly, his thumb brushing over the back of Veer's hand. "It would only make things harder."

"I know," Veer replied, his voice steady despite the turmoil in his heart. "But whatever happens, I'm with you. We'll figure this out together."

They sat there until the last light of the sun faded, their hands still entwined, their bond stronger than ever. For now, words were unnecessary. They had each other, and that was enough.

As the night deepened, they finally stood, their fingers reluctantly parting as they began the walk back to the palace. The road ahead would be difficult, filled with challenges and the expectations of those around them, but they knew they could face it all—because they would face it together.

And in that silent, unspoken promise, they found the courage to keep going, knowing that their love, though hidden, was the strongest weapon they possessed.It gave them the courage to face their challenges and the strength to stand together against any adversities that might come their way.

In the quiet of the night, as they walked side by side, Siddharth and Veer Tej knew that whatever the future held, they would always have each other. Their bond was unbreakable, a connection that went beyond brotherhood and into the realm of something deeper, something eternal.

The chapter of their lives was not without its challenges, especially from those who sought to sow discord. But the love and loyalty they shared were their greatest strengths, forging a connection that would remain unbreakable, no matter what the future held.

As Sam read the chapter, he felt an intense connection to Siddharth and Veer Tej's evolving relationship. Their bond, forged through years of shared experiences, struck a chord deep within him. It wasn't just their friendship that moved him, but the quiet, unspoken love that had grown between them—something that transcended the expectations of their world.

Sam had always been an introvert, guarding his emotions and keeping people at a distance. Yet, in Siddharth and Veer, he saw a reflection of his own unacknowledged longing for a deep, meaningful connection. Their silent understanding, the way they instinctively knew each other's thoughts and feelings, resonated with a part of Sam that he had rarely allowed himself to explore.

The story stirred a mixture of emotions within him. He felt a sense of yearning, an ache for something similar in his own life—someone who could see beyond his reserved exterior and connect with the person he truly was. The chapter also brought a sense of introspection, making him question the walls he had built around himself and whether they were worth the loneliness they caused.

As he finished reading, Sam couldn't help but feel that Siddharth and Veer's story held a deeper significance for him. It wasn't just about a lost kingdom or ancient warriors—it was about understanding the depths of his own desires and the connections he craved. The chapter left him with a quiet resolve, a desire to open himself up to the possibilities of such profound relationships in his own life.

CHAPTER IX

Betrayed by Shadows

Their rivals watched them with eagle eyes, waiting for any slip that could be used against them. The sons of the nobles and ministers, led by the chief minister's son, sought to find fault in the prince and his loyal friend Veer. Despite their efforts to keep their love a secret, whispers and suspicions grew. One day, the chief minister's son, driven by jealousy and ambition, accused Siddharth and Veer of being lovers.

The accusation sent shockwaves throughout the kingdom. The people, who had always admired Siddharth and Veer, found it hard to believe such a scandalous claim. In that era, such an allegation was not only shocking but also a grave matter, carrying severe consequences. The court was in an uproar, and the king was left with no choice but to address the matter publicly.

Siddharth knew that if Veer were called to testify before the king, he would not deny their relationship. Veer's honesty and integrity were unshakeable, and Siddharth feared for his friend's life. The punishment for such an accusation could be dire, possibly even death. Siddharth couldn't bear the thought of Veer being punished, so he devised a plan. He convinced Veer to leave the kingdom temporarily, suggesting that he would take Veer's place in disguise to protect him.

Siddharth placed a reassuring hand on Veer's shoulder. "I have a plan. If you leave the kingdom, I can take your place in disguise. If they discover me, it will buy you enough time to escape."

Veer's gaze met Siddharth's, filled with a mixture of gratitude and sorrow. "You're willing to risk everything for me?"

"I'd do anything to protect you," Siddharth said softly, his eyes intensed with determination. His jaw tightened slightly, revealing the urgency he felt. But beneath the resolve, there was a tenderness in his gaze, a quiet yet fierce love that underscored his words. "But we must act swiftly. The longer we wait, the more dangerous it becomes."

Though Siddharth was certain that his deception would eventually be uncovered, he hoped it would buy Veer enough time to escape. However, their rivals were one step ahead. Before Siddharth could put his plan into action, he was ambushed by the chief minister's son and his cohorts. That night, the storm raged with relentless fury. The rain poured down in torrents, drowning out all other sounds. The world seemed eerily silent, save for the crashing thunder, the crackling lightning, and the relentless drumming of the rain against the earth.

Siddharth, drenched and determined, faced the ten masked assailants with every ounce of strength he could muster. The storm raged around them, but he stood his ground, fighting with relentless courage. Despite his brave resistance, the odds were against him. In a tragic turn of events, a dagger suddenly pierced his chest. Siddharth gasped, blood spilling from his mouth as he staggered and collapsed to the ground.

Even as he lay there, barely conscious, the assailants showed no mercy. One of them swung a heavy log, smashing it against his leg with a sickening crunch. Siddharth's world faded into darkness, the pain overwhelming, but the storm drowned out his agony. The rain and thunder masked the violence, and the night remained eerily silent, as if nothing had happened at all.

As Siddharth lay unconscious, his attackers believed they had killed him. In a panicked effort to conceal their crime, they hastily dug a grave. But as they prepared to bury him, they noticed his hand move slightly. Fearful of being caught, they buried him alive, covering him with earth. Struggling for breath, Siddharth's last thoughts were of Veer, praying for his safety as the earth closed in around him.

Overwhelmed by the horrific scene described in the passage, Sam's emotions broke free. Tears streamed down his face as he cried uncontrollably, his sobs echoing in the silence of the room. The sheer brutality of the incident tore at his heart, leaving him momentarily lost in a sea of sorrow and despair.

He placed his trembling hands on his head, his mind reeling from the cruelty depicted in the words. Images of the scene played in his mind, the pain and helplessness of Siddharth resonating deeply within him. Sam felt a profound connection to the suffering, as if the anguish of that night had crossed the boundaries of time and space to reach him.

For what felt like an eternity, Sam sat there, lost in his grief, unable to shake off the weight of the tragedy. His mind spiraled into dark thoughts, questioning the nature of humanity and the capacity for such violence. The world seemed to close in around him, the room shrinking as his emotions threatened to consume him.

But slowly, as the tears subsided and his breathing steadied, Sam began to regain his composure. He wiped his face with a shaking hand, trying to push the overwhelming sorrow aside. With a heavy heart, he knew he had to continue. There was more to this story, more to uncover and understand.

Taking a deep breath, Sam returned his focus to the passage. Though his heart still ached, he found the strength to continue reading, determined to piece together the story that had affected him so deeply. The cruel incident had shaken him to his core, but it also fueled his resolve to uncover the truth and honor the memory of those who had suffered.

Meanwhile, Veer, true to his nature, couldn't bring himself to flee. He faced the king, confessing the truth about their love.

In the grand hall, his voice was resolute despite the turmoil around him. "Your Majesty, I must confess the truth. Siddharth and I—our bond is indeed as the rumors say. But it is true love, not a betrayal. Please, spare him and judge me instead." He begged the king to spare Siddharth, willing to accept any punishment.

The revelation stunned the court into silence. The king, torn between his duty and his love for his son, was unable to respond immediately. Veer's father, Captain Tej, stood in the corner, his face twisted in rage and shame. Unable to bear the dishonor, he seized the moment in a fit of fury, executing Veer before the court's helpless gaze.

The horror in the hall was palpable as Veer's lifeless body was revealed. The king, his face a mask of anguish and fury, struggled to maintain his composure. The once-silent hall erupted into chaos, filled with gasps and cries of disbelief as the brutal reality of the tragedy unfolded before their eyes.

Regaining his composure, the king ordered the captain's arrest, condemning him for taking justice into his own hands. He then commanded his men to search for Siddharth, desperate to find his son.

For two agonizing days, they scoured the kingdom, but Siddharth was nowhere to be found. Finally, one of the conspirators, guilt- ridden and fearful of divine retribution, confessed to the crime. The entire kingdom was horrified by the brutal murder of their beloved prince.

In a heart-wrenching ceremony, the king laid his son to rest with all the honors he could muster, choosing a place that Siddharth had cherished. However, due to the sensitive nature of the events and the potential for defamation, the king decided to conceal the truth. The tomb's location remained a closely guarded secret, known only to a few. Veer was cremated with traditional rituals, mourned deeply by those who had loved him.

To address the treachery, the chief minister's son and the other conspirators were sentenced to death. Their betrayal not only led to a tragic end for the young prince and his friend but also left an indelible stain on the kingdom's history. The execution of the conspirators served as a harsh reminder of the consequences of such treachery, and their actions were condemned as a dark chapter in an otherwise golden era.

In the wake of these tragedies, the kingdom was left without a male heir. After the King's demise, the queen, heartbroken but resolute, took on the mantle of leadership. She ruled with wisdom and compassion, preserving peace and stability. However, without the strength and unity once symbolized by Siddharth and Veer, the kingdom gradually declined. The golden era faded into memory, leaving behind a legacy of love, sacrifice, and loss.

The stories of the prince and his loyal companion became legends, passed down through generations, a poignant reminder of the price of love in a world bound by tradition and prejudice.

With a shaky breath, Sam realized that he could not face any more of the story that night. He was broken, shattered by the brutality and loss, unable to bear the thought of reading another word. Slowly, he stood up, his legs weak and unsteady, and left the room, seeking solace in the quiet darkness of the night.

CHAPTER X

Unveiling the Portrait

Next day, Sam sat in stunned silence, the weight of the story's tragedy pressing heavily upon him. His eyes remained fixed on the pages, though they barely registered the words. The details of Siddharth's fate—buried alive, struggling for breath as the cold earth enveloped him—struck a visceral chord within him. Sam's mind whirled with images of Siddharth's desperate gasps for air, his heart pounding in a frantic rhythm, and the suffocating darkness closing in.

The thought of Veer's beheading, executed without even a moment's pause for understanding or reconciliation, left him feeling hollow. The brutal and senseless violence unfolded before his eyes, a stark contrast to the loyalty and affection the two had shared. The horror of Veer's final moments, met with shock and disbelief by the court, echoed in Sam's thoughts like a relentless drumbeat.

As the gravity of the events sank in, Sam felt an almost physical jolt of anguish. His head felt as if it were spinning out of control, overwhelmed by the enormity of the loss and the cruelty of fate. The story had shattered his sense of reality, leaving him grappling with a profound sorrow and disbelief. The tragedy of Siddharth and Veer's demise, so starkly illustrated in the pages, had a disorienting effect, as if the world he had known had been irrevocably altered by the depth of their suffering.

His hands shook as he hesitated to close the book, feeling a strange compulsion to keep reading. It was then that he noticed there was one more page. Curiosity, mingled with a sense of dread, drove him to turn it.

What Sam saw next left him breathless. The page revealed an illustration of Prince Siddharth and Veer Tej, rendered in exquisite detail. The image captured the essence of their bond, showing them standing side by side with expressions of camaraderie and affection.

But what truly shocked Sam was the face of Veer Tej. The resemblance was more than striking—it was unnerving. Every detail of Veer Tej's face seemed to mirror his own, from the shape of his jawline to the set of his eyes. It was as though he was looking into a reflection of himself from another era, his breath hitching as the reality of the similarity hit him.

Sam's mind went blank. The world around him seemed to collapse into a single, intense focus on the portrait. The uncanny likeness left him reeling, his thoughts swirling in a maelstrom of disbelief and confusion. It wasn't merely a resemblance; it was a mirror image that defied logical explanation.

In the midst of his shock, a strange, involuntary reaction occurred. Sam's eyes widened, and his mouth fell open in an expression of utter bewilderment. He touched his head and face, as if to ensure they were still there, feeling an almost comical sense of disconnection from reality. He shook his head vigorously, trying to snap himself out of what felt like a surreal, otherworldly experience . He felt like he was in the middle of a bizarre dream, where the boundaries of reality and fiction had blurred beyond recognition. His gaze remained fixed on the portrait, his emotions a tangled mess of awe and dread. The image of Veer Tej, so hauntingly similar to himself, stirred a flood of questions.

Could he be a reincarnation of this ancient figure? Was this extraordinary resemblance merely a peculiar coincidence, or was it a sign pointing toward something far more profound?

The realization struck Sam with a sudden, almost comic force. He could feel the corners of his lips twitching, as if they were on the verge of breaking into a bewildered grin. His brain struggled to process the absurdity of the situation. He imagined himself in a comedy sketch, where the seriousness of the revelation was undermined by his own incredulous reaction. The contrast between his internal turmoil and the bizarre nature of the revelation created a surreal, almost absurdly funny moment.

Sam's thoughts raced in disjointed fragments. "Is this some kind of cosmic joke?" he wondered, his mind struggling to reconcile the seriousness of the historical tragedy with the ludicrous idea that he might be linked to it. He felt a strange mixture of fear, amusement, and disbelief. His face flushed, his eyes darting between the portrait and the room around him, as if expecting someone to jump out and shout, "Surprise!"

The weight of the book in his hands felt oddly comforting now, like an anchor to reality that had slipped away. Sam's mind, though still shaken, found a peculiar solace in the absurdity of his reaction. He took a deep breath, trying to ground himself in the present moment, his mind slowly beginning to clear.

With shaky hands, he closed the book, the portrait of Veer Tej staring back at him even as the cover was shut. He needed to process what he had seen, to make sense of the strange connection that had been revealed. The book lay heavy in his lap, a silent testament to the bizarre intersection of his life with the tragic past of Siddharth and

Veer.

As he sat there, trying to steady his breath and regain his composure, Sam couldn't help but let out a soft, incredulous laugh. The situation was so fantastical that it bordered on the absurd. He knew he had to confront the implications of this revelation, but for now, the sheer strangeness of the discovery was enough to leave him in a state of stunned, bewildered reflection.

The weight of these revelations pressed heavily on Sam's chest, making him feel emotionally unwell. His head spun with the implications, each thought crashing into the next as he struggled to piece together the truth. The portrait had unearthed a connection to a past life, opening a door to mysteries he had only begun to explore.

With a trembling hand, Sam closed the book, the image of Veer Tej's face lingering vividly in his mind. The journey he had undertaken had taken a personal and haunting turn, intertwining his fate with the tragic figures from history in ways he could scarcely comprehend. Driven by the urgent need for answers, Sam resolved to dive deeper into the ancient texts and artifacts, determined to unravel the mysteries that linked him to the souls of Siddharth and Veer Tej.

CHAPTER XI

Unveiling the Truth

After the archaeological team's discovery, the forensic department took charge of analyzing the excavated remains, including the ancient mummy. The forensic experts conducted a series of comprehensive tests to determine the age, cause of death, and other critical details.

The initial tests revealed that the mummy was approximately five hundred sixty-nine years old. This determination was based on radiocarbon dating of the embalming materials and the organic remains.

One of the most significant findings was that the individual had been embalmed roughly two days after death. This was deduced from the state of preservation of the body and the embalming materials used. The presence of specific chemicals and the condition of the tissue indicated that embalming occurred in a relatively short period following death.

The cause of death and the condition of the body provided further insights into the individual's final moments. Forensic analysis uncovered that the individual had sustained multiple injuries before death. Here are the key findings:

Wounds Consistent with Sword-like Objects: The body had twelve large wounds consistent with sword-like objects. These were identified through the examination of cut marks and the depth of the injuries. The pattern and severity of the wounds suggested a violent assault with a bladed weapon.

Broken Ribs and Dagger Injury: The individual's left ribs were fractured, indicating a severe impact, likely from a dagger or similar pointed weapon. The forensic team identified these injuries by examining the fracture patterns and comparing them with known trauma caused by blunt and sharp objects.

Amputation of Fingers: The right four fingers had been severed, a detail determined through the analysis of the bone structure and the presence of clean-cut surfaces. This type of injury suggested a deliberate act of dismemberment, possibly as a form of punishment or torture.

Broken Leg: The right leg was found to be fractured. The type of fracture, along with the position of the break, indicated that it was caused by a blunt force impact, such as a blow or a heavy object.

Evidence of Being Buried Alive: The forensic team identified signs that the individual had been buried alive. This conclusion was drawn from several observations:

Airway Obstruction: The position of the body and the state of the lungs indicated that the individual was still breathing or struggling to breathe when buried.

Signs of Struggle: The wounds and fractures, combined with the disorganized position of the body, suggested a final struggle. The individual's attempts to escape or fight back before death might have led to these injuries.

Embalming Timing: The embalming was performed relatively two days after the injuries, suggesting that the individual might have been alive at the time of the burial and subsequently preserved to delay decomposition.

The forensic findings painted a grim picture of the individual's final moments. At only nineteen years old, the individual had suffered severe injuries and was buried alive, highlighting a tragic end to a young life.Adding to the mystery, the body had a distinctive black scar shaped like a butterfly on the left hand. This unique mark linked the deceased to the narratives Sam had been uncovering, intensifying the emotional impact.

Sam was deeply affected by the revelations. His heart felt heavy, as though it might break at any moment. The thought of the immense pain and suffering the young individual had endured left him devastated. He couldn't move, frozen by the weight of the tragic details.

The detailed scientific analysis not only provided clarity about the past but also connected the ancient mysteries to his ongoing quest. The vivid imagery of the injuries and the thought of being buried alive haunted him. It was as if he could feel the echoes of the past's agony and turmoil within himself.

The final piece of the puzzle came as a shock: the body they had discovered was none other than that of Prince Siddharth, the cherished child of King Karthikeya and Queen Suvarna. The distinctive butterfly-shaped scar on the left hand confirmed this heartbreaking revelation. The realization that the prince, who had been so beloved and celebrated in the kingdom's history, had met such a gruesome end was overwhelming for Sam. It shattered the idyllic image he had formed from the earlier stories and brought the reality of the Prince's tragic fate into sharp, painful focus.

The more Sam learned, the more he felt driven to uncover the full story behind these harrowing events. The revelations stirred a profound sense of purpose in him, compelling him to dig deeper into the mysteries of the past and the role he might play in resolving them. He knew there was more to this tale, and he felt a deep, almost personal responsibility to bring the truth to light. The story of Prince Siddharth's life and death became a mission for Sam, as he sought to piece together the events that led to such a devastating conclusion.

CHAPTER XII

The Grand Finale: A Hilarious Twist

Sam was dumbfounded, grappling with the realization that he was the reincarnation of Veer Tej and that Prince Siddharth had been calling out to him all these years, guiding him to reveal this hidden story to the world. As he absorbed this monumental truth, his phone rang.

The office's name flashed on the screen, pulling him from his reverie.

"Hello, this is Sam," he answered, his voice distracted.

"Hi, Sam, this is Julie from the office. I just wanted to remind you that your new assistant will be joining you tomorrow," Julie's voice came through, clear and professional.

"Right, right. Thanks for the reminder," Sam replied absently, struggling to focus.

"He's a rookie, but very eager to learn. Should be interesting to have him around," Julie continued, oblivious to Sam's preoccupation.

"Sure, I'll be sure to give him a warm welcome," Sam said, barely registering the words.

"Great. Also, he's on his way over now to get acquainted before his first day. Thought you might want to know," Julie added.

"Okay, thanks for letting me know," Sam mumbled, his mind still entangled in the revelations he'd just uncovered.

"Alright, see you tomorrow. Take care," Julie said, wrapping up the call.

"Yeah, see you," Sam replied, barely hearing the goodbye. He hung up just as the doorbell rang, the sound jolting him further into the present.

Feeling a mix of curiosity and unease, Sam shuffled to the door. As he opened it, his jaw dropped. Standing before him was a young man who looked like Prince Siddharth had just stepped out of a time machine and into the present. Clad in modern attire, this Siddharth was the spitting image of the ancient prince. Astonished, he blinked rapidly, half-expecting to wake up from what seemed like an elaborate dream.

"Hi! I'm Siddharth, your new assistant!" the young man said cheerfully, extending his left hand for a handshake. He was all smiles and bright-eyed enthusiasm.

Sam's eyes widened even further as he noticed the butterfly-shaped scar on Siddharth's left hand—the same mark he'd seen in the ancient texts and on the mummy. The realization hit him with the force of a freight train: Siddharth, his new assistant, was a dead ringer for the prince from the story. Sam felt the room tilt, his mind spinning like a top. Was this some sort of cosmic prank? A divine joke? He wasn't sure, but he was on the verge of collapsing from the sheer absurdity.

As Sam swayed on his feet, struggling to maintain his balance, Siddharth quickly stepped forward, catching him with the ease of someone who had clearly done this before. "Whoa, are you okay, sir?" Siddharth asked, his face a picture of concern. "You look like you've seen a ghost!"

Sam managed a weak, lopsided smile, struggling to suppress a laugh. "You... you wouldn't believe me if I told you," he stammered, still staring at the scar like it was some sort of supernatural artifact.

Siddharth glanced at his hand, then back at Sam, a puzzled look on his face. "It's just a birthmark," he said with a shrug, clearly bemused. "Nothing special. But you look like I've just handed you a cursed relic!"

Sam couldn't help but chuckle at the irony. "You have no idea," he muttered, still trying to wrap his head around the hilarity of the situation. Here he was, face-to-face with what could only be described as a reincarnation of Prince Siddharth, who had somehow ended up as his assistant.

As they settled in, Siddharth proved to be as enthusiastic and eager as any rookie could be. His youthful energy and eagerness to learn were refreshing, but every so often, Sam found himself staring, half-expecting Siddharth to start talking about ancient kingdoms or reveal a hidden treasure.

But no, Siddharth was just a regular young man with no clue about the cosmic coincidence that had brought him to Sam's doorstep. And perhaps that was the most hilarious part of it all—the idea that, after all the mystical revelations and ancient secrets, Sam's grand, supernatural saga had ended with a simple, modern twist.

As days passed, the strange synchronicity of their meeting faded into the background. Siddharth turned out to be a competent assistant, and Sam found himself laughing at the absurdity of the situation more than anything else. He never experienced another time slip after that day, and the ancient mysteries seemed to settle into a quiet corner of his mind, content with having been revealed.

Sam often looked at Siddharth, chuckling at the thought of the cosmic prank the universe had played on him. Maybe it was fate, destiny, or just a weird coincidence. Whatever it was, it had made for a story he would never forget—a story that began with an ancient artifact and ended with a rookie assistant who just happened to share a name and a scar with a prince from the past.

And so, Sam's extraordinary journey concluded not with a dramatic climax but with a light-hearted twist, a reminder that sometimes life's most profound moments come wrapped in the most unexpected, and hilarious, packages.

Sam stood by his desk, the ancient book of the lost kingdom in one hand and a file containing the documents in the other. He glanced at Siddharth, who was busy organizing some papers. Sam had been mulling over this decision for a while, and now, it felt like the right time.

Clearing his throat, Sam caught Siddharth's attention. "Siddharth," he began, his voice steady but laced with a hint of the weight he felt. "There's something I want you to take a look at."

Siddharth looked up, curious. "Sure, what is it, sir?"

Sam hesitated for a moment, then extended the book and the file toward him. "This," he said, "is the book I've been reading. It's about an ancient kingdom, and... well, it's not just any book. And these documents—there's a lot tied to them. I think you should have a look."

Siddharth's eyes widened in surprise as he took the items from Sam. "Are you sure, sir? This seems... important."

"It is," Sam replied, nodding slowly. "I've been doing a lot of thinking, and I believe you might be the right person to help me with this. I can't explain it all right now, but let's just say this book might have answers to questions I didn't even know I had. And the file—it contains details that are... relevant."

Siddharth looked down at the book, then back at Sam, sensing the gravity of the moment. "I'll go through it carefully," he said, his tone serious. "But what exactly am I looking for?"

Sam paused, trying to find the right words. "You're looking for anything that feels... familiar. Anything that resonates with you. Trust your instincts on this, Siddharth. There's more to this than meets the eye."

Siddharth nodded, though he couldn't quite hide the puzzled expression on his face. "I'll do my best, sir. But, if you don't mind me asking—why me? I'm just your assistant, and this seems like something... well, something way beyond my expertise."

Sam smiled faintly. "I can't explain it fully, not yet. But I have a feeling you're more connected to this than you realize. Just take your time with it. We'll figure it out together."

Siddharth's confusion deepened, but he nodded, sensing that Sam wasn't ready to divulge everything just yet. "Okay, I'll start going through it tonight. And if I find anything, you'll be the first to know."

"Thank you, Siddharth," Sam said, feeling a strange mix of relief and anticipation. "And remember—don't overthink it. Just let yourself be open to whatever you might find."

Siddharth gave a reassuring smile. "I'll keep that in mind, sir. And, for what it's worth, I'm glad you trust me with this."

Sam nodded, watching as Siddharth left the room with the book and file in hand. A part of him felt lighter, as if a burden had been shared. But another part of him knew that this was just the beginning of something much bigger.

And Who knows, Perhaps in the grand theater of life, they might just find love again, rewriting history in a new, modern chapter. Only time would tell.

The Unmapped

As Sam deciphered the manuscript, a chilling statement below the title caught his eye: "Whoever reads this book will be cursed." It was an unsettling warning, clearly intended to deter anyone from uncovering the secrets within. Despite the foreboding message, Sam felt an irresistible pull to continue, driven by an unshakeable need to unearth the truth.

The manuscript, penned in a long-forgotten script and hidden within the royal archives, had been shielded from history by a royal edict. Thanks to advanced software, Sam had managed to decipher its delicate text, revealing a story that transcended time and official accounts. This secret record of love, betrayal, and tragedy, so poignantly detailed, was now unveiled, its authenticity underscored by its rich narrative.

As Sam reached the end of the manuscript, the purpose of the ominous warning became clear. It was not a literal curse but a deliberate deterrent crafted to keep the book's contents concealed. The court poet, who had written this manuscript, had used the warning to prevent the revelation of the story's tragic details.

The poet wrote: "Today, I witnessed a heart-wrenching incident, one that will stay with me for a long time. This is the story that unfolded before my eyes, a tale of raw emotion and the fragility of the human spirit. I write this account as a secret, to be kept in the Court library among hidden records. What I am doing is forbidden, as the court has decreed that this event must never be included in the official history of the Empire. Officially, it is recorded that Siddharth and Veer Tej succumbed to an unknown disease that plagued our land. But the truth is far more sorrowful, and it is this truth that I now commit to these pages."

For six centuries, the manuscript had remained buried in the archives, safeguarded by the curse warning that effectively deterred readers. The truth about Prince Siddharth and Veer Tej had been obscured, both literally and metaphorically, preserved behind a fabricated history.

The revelation that Siddharth, the new assistant, not only shared the name of the ancient prince but also bore a butterfly-shaped scar identical to the one described in the manuscript, left Sam with a profound sense of connection and confusion. The resemblance and the scar mirrored those of the historical figure, making the discovery both startling and poignant.

The more Sam pondered the curse, the more he understood why the story had been hidden for so long. It was a mechanism to keep the truth buried and the kingdom's carefully crafted facade intact. The legacy of Siddharth and Veer Tej had remained in the shadows, guarded by a curse designed to prevent discovery.

As he reflected on the possibility of reincarnation, Sam grappled with the notion that his discovery might not be mere coincidence but part of a larger cosmic plan. The idea that he could be linked to a past life through this narrative felt disturbingly real, challenging his understanding of fate and identity.

The manuscript's revelations left Sam with a mixture of awe and apprehension. Some mysteries, he realized, might never be fully understood. The story of Siddharth and Veer Tej, and his own strange connection to it, transcended time and logic. It was a reminder that life often holds more mysteries than we can comprehend, urging us to navigate the unknown with curiosity and wonder.

As the final page of "The Unmapped" turned, Sam embraced the possibility that he might never have all the answers. The manuscript, hidden for six centuries, had finally brought its secrets into the light, offering a glimpse into a past that felt surprisingly close and a future brimming with possibilities. With a sense of trepidation and hope, Sam resolved to accept whatever came next, recognizing that love and history are intricately connected across lifetimes.